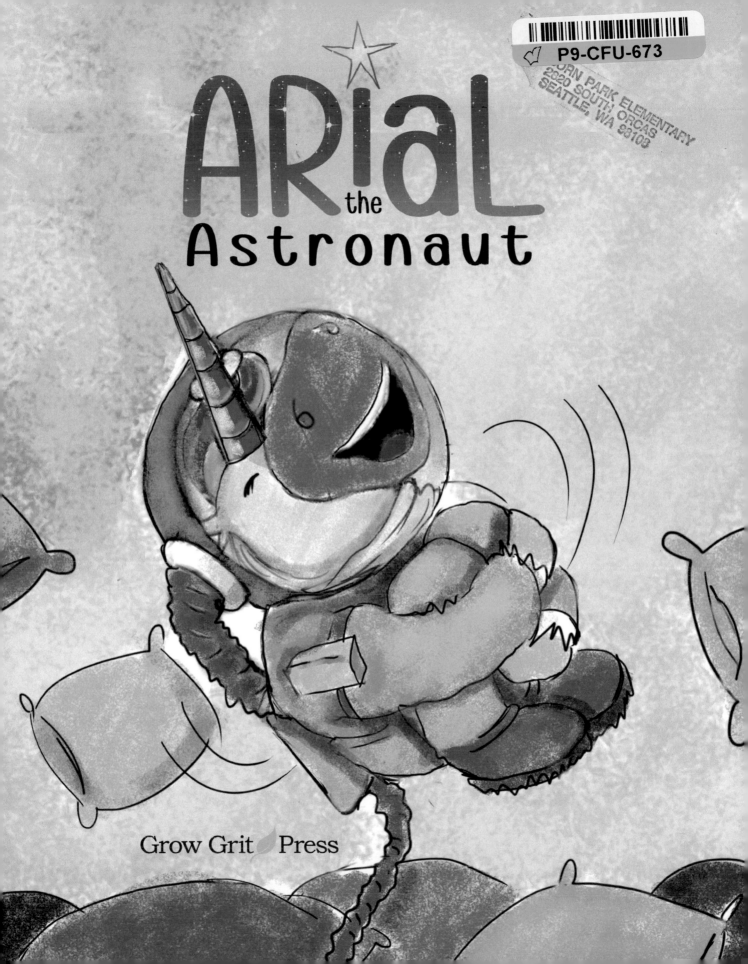

ARiAL the Astronaut

Grow Grit Press

For school and book signings/readings, email marynhin@gmail.com
ISBN 978-1-951056-96-4

Cataloging in Publication Data Library of Congress Control number: 2019907622
Printed and bound in the USA. First printing June 2019
UnicornPreneur.com

This book is dedicated to my nieces and nephew:

Arielle, Aileen, and Alex.

Tuesday is a day much like any other day for **Arial**.

Aliens and astronauts.
Astronauts and aliens!

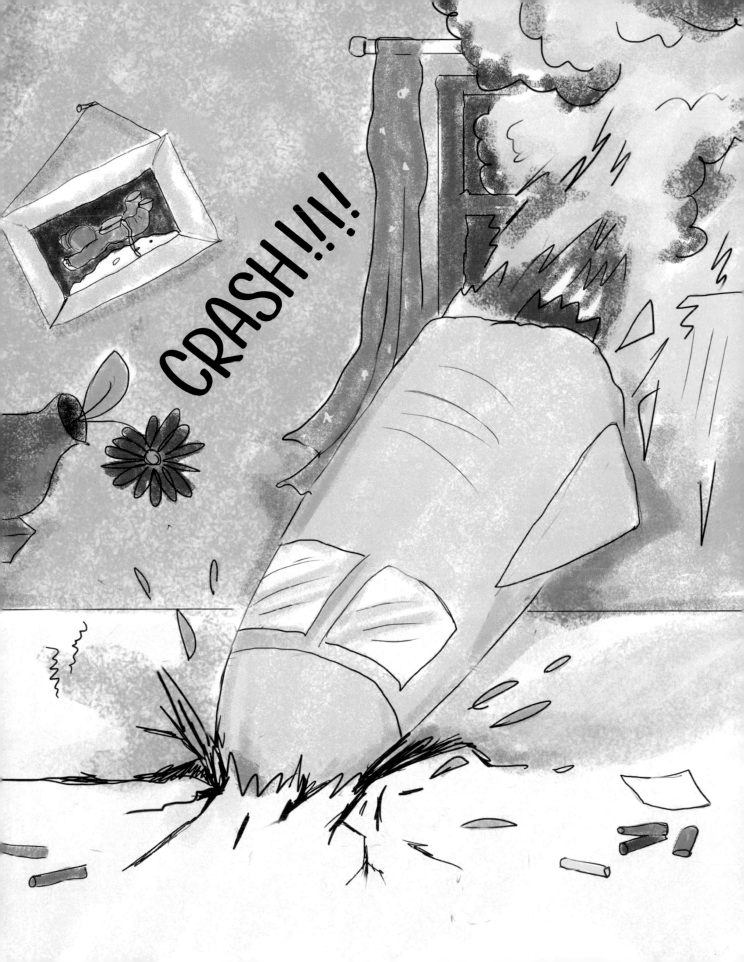

Arial shouts,
"Look at my flips!"

"Planets Mars and Venus up ahead," announces the pilot.

"Venus is glowing!"
exclaims Arial.

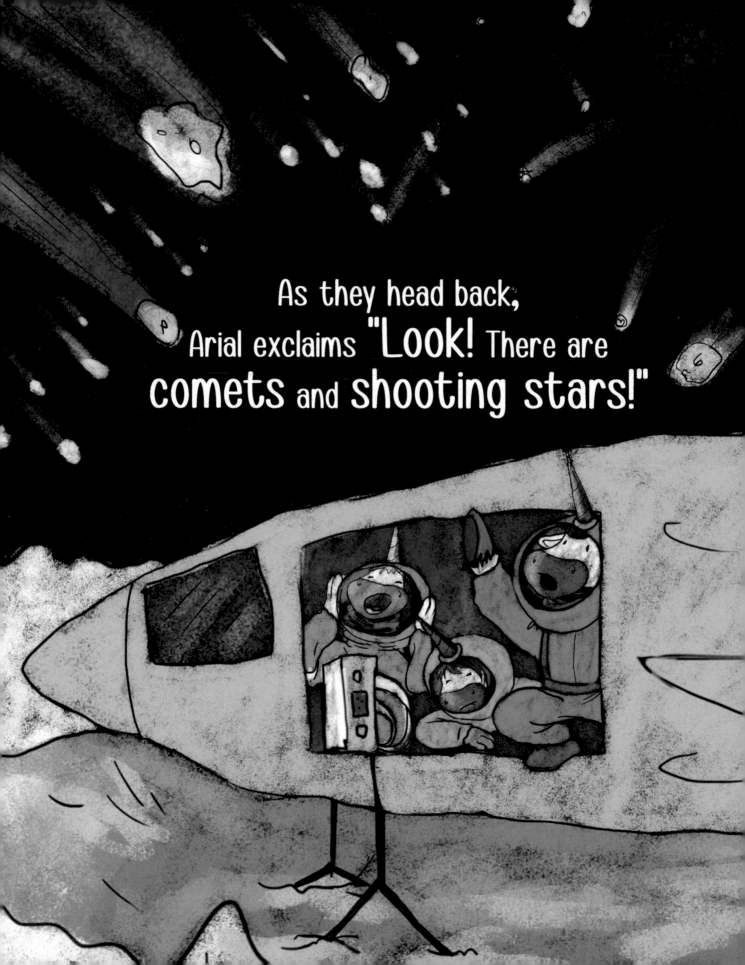

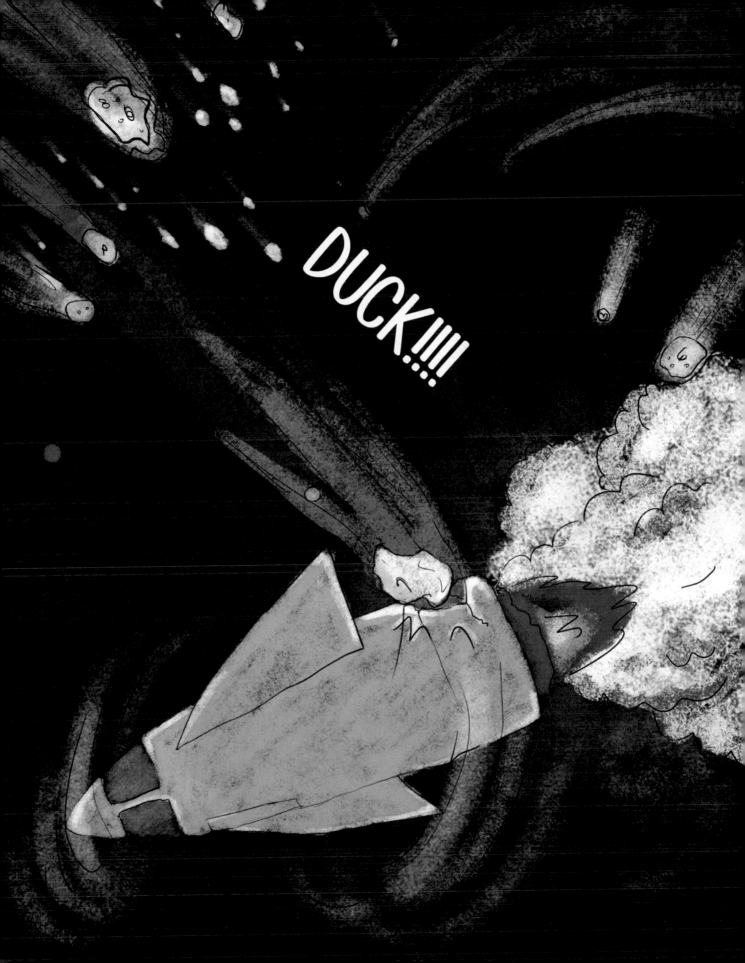

"If I can just get this control unstuck..." says **Arial**.

Arial **maneuvers** some wires and **creates** a special tool to loosen the stuck control.

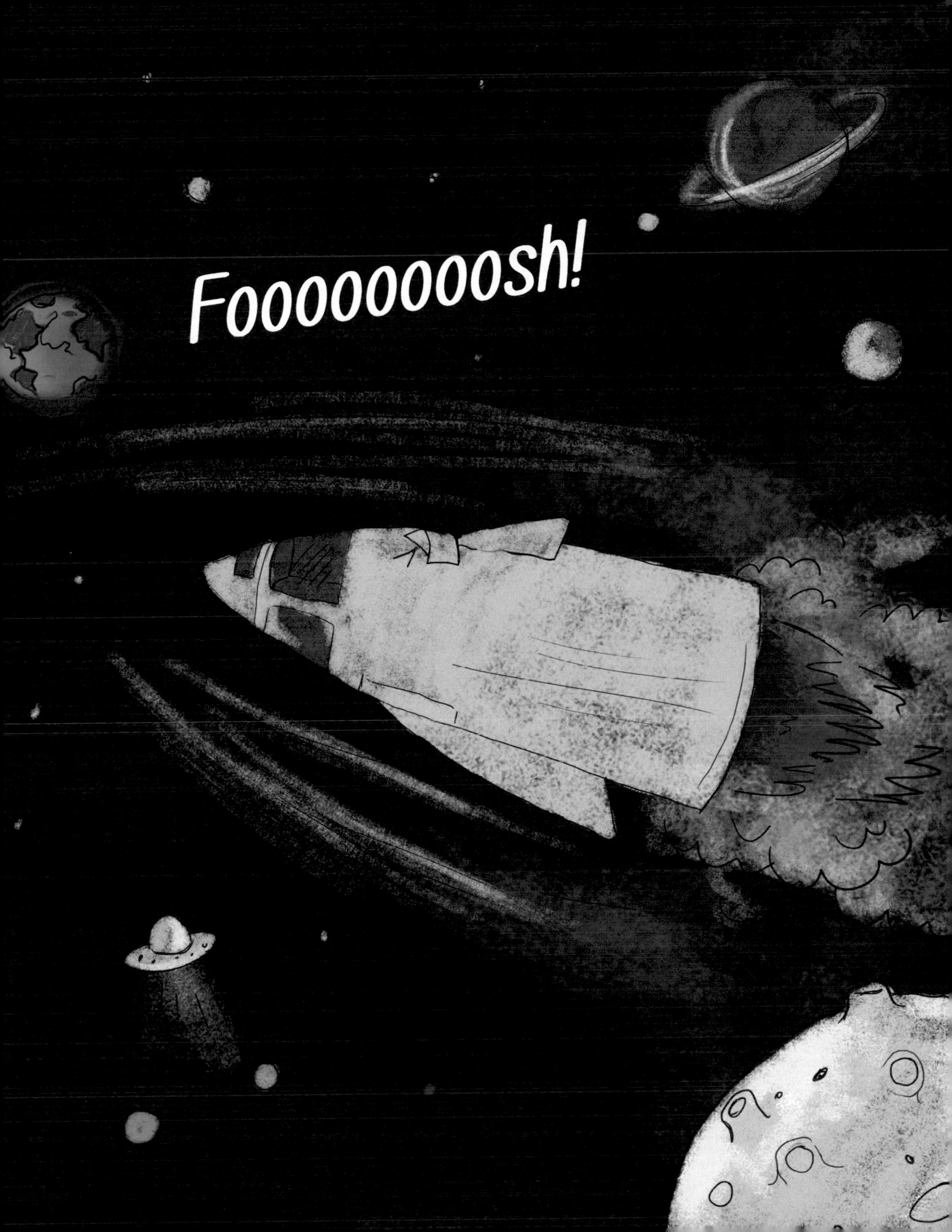
Fooooooooosh!

The End

UnicornPreneur
Series

Made in the USA
Monee, IL
01 December 2020